THE DIAMOND AS BIG AS THE RITZ

THE DIAMOND AS BIG AS THE RITZ

F. Scott Fitzgerald

❧Juniper Grove❧

ISBN 978-1-60355-105-2
©2008 Juniper Grove

Author's Preface

"The Diamond as Big as the Ritz," which appeared last summer in the *Smart Set*, was designed utterly for my own amusement. I was in that familiar mood characterized by a perfect craving for luxury, and the story began as an attempt to feed that craving on imaginary foods.

One well-known critic has been pleased to like this extravaganza better than anything I have written. Personally I prefer "The Off Shore Pirate." But, to tamper slightly with Lincoln: If you like this sort of thing, this, possibly, is the sort of thing you'll like.

F. Scott Fitzgerald
1922

THE DIAMOND AS BIG AS THE RITZ

1

John T. Unger came from a family that had been well known in Hades—a small town on the Mississippi River—for several generations. John's father had held the amateur golf championship through many a heated contest; Mrs. Unger was known "from hot-box to hot-bed," as the local phrase went, for her political addresses; and young John T. Unger, who had just turned sixteen, had danced all the latest dances from New York before he put on long trousers. And now, for a certain time, he was to be away from home. That respect for a New England education which is the bane of all provincial places, which drains them yearly of their most promising young men, had seized upon his parents. Nothing would suit them but that he should go to St. Midas' School near Boston—Hades was too small to hold their darling and gifted son.

Now in Hades—as you know if you ever have been there—the names of the more fashionable preparatory schools and colleges mean very little. The inhabitants have been so long out of the world that, though they make a show of keeping up-to-date in dress and manners and literature, they depend to a great extent on hearsay, and a function that in Hades would be considered elaborate would doubtless be hailed by a Chicago beef-princess as "perhaps a little tacky."

John T. Unger was on the eve of departure. Mrs. Unger, with maternal fatuity, packed his trunks full of linen suits and electric fans, and Mr. Unger presented his son with an asbestos pocket-book stuffed with money.

"Remember, you are always welcome here," he said. "You can be sure, boy, that we'll keep the home fires burning."

"I know," answered John huskily.

"Don't forget who you are and where you come from," continued his father proudly, "and you can do nothing to harm you. You are an Unger—from Hades."

So the old man and the young shook hands and John walked away with tears streaming from his eyes. Ten minutes later he had passed outside the city limits, and he stopped to glance back for the last time. Over the gates the old-fashioned Victorian motto seemed strangely attractive to him. His father had tried time and time again to have it changed to something with a little more push and verve about it, such as "Hades—Your Opportunity," or else a plain "Welcome" sign set over a hearty handshake pricked out in electric lights. The old motto was a little depressing, Mr. Unger had thought—but now....

So John took his look and then set his face resolutely toward his destination. And, as he turned away, the lights of Hades against the sky seemed full of a warm and passionate beauty.

St. Midas' School is half an hour from Boston in a Rolls-Pierce motor-car. The actual distance will never be known, for no one, except John T. Unger, had ever arrived there save in a Rolls-Pierce and probably no one ever will again. St. Midas' is the most expensive and the most exclusive boys' preparatory school in the world.

John's first two years there passed pleasantly. The fathers of all the boys were money-kings and John spent his summer visiting at fashionable resorts. While he was very fond of all the boys he visited, their fathers struck him as being much of a piece, and in his boyish way he often wondered at their exceeding sameness. When he told them where his home was they would ask jovially, "Pretty hot down there?" and John would muster a faint smile and answer, "It certainly is." His response would have been heartier had they not all made this joke—at best varying it with, "Is it hot enough for you down there?" which he hated just as much.

In the middle of his second year at school, a quiet, handsome boy named Percy Washington had been put in John's form. The newcomer was pleasant in his manner and exceedingly well dressed even for St. Midas', but for some reason he kept aloof from the other boys. The only person with whom he was intimate was John T. Unger, but even to John he was entirely uncommunicative concerning his home or his family. That he was wealthy went without saying, but beyond a few such deductions John knew little of his friend, so it promised rich confectionery for his curiosity when Percy invited him to spend the summer at his home "in the West." He accepted, without hesitation.

It was only when they were in the train that Percy became, for the first time, rather communicative. One day while they were eating lunch in the dining-car and discussing the imperfect characters of several of the boys at school, Percy suddenly changed his tone and made an abrupt remark.

"My father," he said, "is by far the richest man in the world."

"Oh," said John politely. He could think of no answer to make to this confidence. He considered "That's very nice," but it sounded hollow and was on the point of saying, "Really?" but refrained since it would seem to question Percy's statement. And such an astounding statement could scarcely be questioned.

"By far the richest," repeated Percy.

"I was reading in the *World Almanac*," began John, "that there was one man in America with an income of over five million a year and four men with incomes of over three million a year, and——"

"Oh, they're nothing." Percy's mouth was a half-moon of scorn. "Catch-penny capitalists, financial small-fry, petty merchants and money-lenders. My father could buy them out and not know he'd done it."

"But how does he——"

"Why haven't they put down *his* income tax? Because he doesn't pay any. At least he pays a little one—but he doesn't pay any on his *real* income.

"He must be very rich," said John simply. "I'm glad. I like very rich people."

"The richer a fella is, the better I like him." There was a look of passionate frankness upon his dark face. "I visited the Schnlitzer-Murphys last Easter. Vivian Schnlitzer-Murphy had rubies as big as hen's eggs, and sapphires that were like globes with lights inside them——"

"I love jewels," agreed Percy enthusiastically. "Of course I wouldn't want anyone at school to know about it, but I've got quite a collection myself. I used to collect them instead of stamps."

"And diamonds," continued John eagerly. "The Schnlitzer-Murphys had diamonds as big as walnuts——"

"That's nothing." Percy had leaned forward and dropped his voice to a low whisper. "That's nothing at all. My father has a diamond bigger than the Ritz-Carlton Hotel."

2

The Montana sunset lay between two mountains like a gigantic bruise from which dark arteries spread themselves over a poisoned sky. An immense distance under the sky crouched the village of Fish, minute, dismal, and forgotten. There were twelve men, so it was said, in the village of Fish, twelve sombre and inexplicable souls who sucked a lean milk from the almost literally bare rock upon which a mysterious populatory force had begotten them. They had become a race apart, these twelve men of Fish, like some species developed by an early whim of nature, which on second thought had abandoned them to struggle and extermination.

Out of the blue-black bruise in the distance crept a long line of moving lights upon the desolation of the land, and the twelve men of Fish gathered like ghosts at the shanty depot to watch the passing of the seven o'clock train, the Transcontinental Express from Chicago. Six times or so a year the Transcontinental Express, through some inconceivable jurisdiction, stopped at the village of Fish, and when this occurred a figure or so would disembark, mount into a buggy that always appeared from out of the dusk, and drive off toward the bruised sunset. The observation of this pointless and preposterous phenomenon had become a sort of cult among the men of Fish. To observe, that was all; there remained in them none of the vital quality of illusion which would make them wonder or speculate, else a religion might have grown up around these mysterious visitations. But the men of Fish were beyond all religion—the barest and most savage tenets of even Christianity could gain no foothold on that barren rock—so there was no altar, no priest, no sacrifice; only each night at seven the silent concourse by the shanty depot, a congregation who lifted up a prayer of dim, anaemic wonder.

On this June night, the Great Brakeman, whom, had they deified anyone, they might well have chosen as their celestial protagonist, had ordained that the seven o'clock train should leave its human (or inhuman) deposit at Fish. At two minutes after seven Percy Washington and John T. Unger disembarked, hurried past the spellbound, the agape, the fearsome eyes of the twelve men of Fish, mounted into a buggy which had obviously appeared from nowhere, and drove away.

After half an hour, when the twilight had coagulated into dark, the silent negro who was driving the buggy hailed an opaque body somewhere ahead of them in the gloom. In response to his cry, it turned upon them a luminous disc which regarded them like a malignant eye out of the unfathomable night. As they came closer, John saw that it was the tail-light of an immense automobile, larger and more magnificent than any he had ever seen. Its body was of gleaming metal richer than nickel and lighter than silver, and the hubs of the wheels were studded with iridescent geometric figures of green and yellow—John did not dare to guess whether they were glass or jewel.

Two negroes, dressed in glittering livery such as one sees in pictures of royal processions in London, were standing at attention beside the car and as the two young men dismounted from the buggy they were greeted in some language which the guest could not understand, but which seemed to be an extreme form of the Southern negro's dialect.

"Get in," said Percy to his friend, as their trunks were tossed to the ebony roof of the limousine. "Sorry we had to bring you this far in that buggy, but of course it wouldn't do for the people on the train or those God-forsaken fellas in Fish to see this automobile."

"Gosh! What a car!" This ejaculation was provoked by its interior. John saw that the upholstery consisted of a thousand minute and exquisite tapestries of silk, woven with jewels and embroideries, and set upon a background of cloth of gold. The two armchair seats in which the boys luxuriated were covered with stuff that resembled duvetyn, but seemed woven in numberless colors of the ends of ostrich feathers.

"What a car!" cried John again, in amazement.

"This thing?" Percy laughed. "Why, it's just an old junk we use for a station wagon."

By this time they were gliding along through the darkness toward the break between the two mountains.

"We'll be there in an hour and a half," said Percy, looking at the clock. "I may as well tell you it's not going to be like anything you ever saw before."

If the car was any indication of what John would see, he was prepared to be astonished indeed. The simple piety prevalent in Hades has the earnest worship of and respect for riches as the first article of its creed—had John felt otherwise than radiantly humble before them, his parents would have turned away in horror at the blasphemy.

They had now reached and were entering the break between the two mountains and almost immediately the way became much rougher.

"If the moon shone down here, you'd see that we're in a big gulch," said Percy, trying to peer out of the window. He spoke a few words into the mouthpiece and immediately the footman turned on a searchlight and swept the hillsides with an immense beam.

"Rocky, you see. An ordinary car would be knocked to pieces in half an hour. In fact, it'd take a tank to navigate it unless you knew the way. You notice we're going uphill now."

They were obviously ascending, and within a few minutes the car was crossing a high rise, where they caught a glimpse of a pale moon newly risen in the distance. The car stopped suddenly and several figures took shape out of the dark beside it—these were negroes also. Again the two young men were saluted in the same dimly recognizable dialect; then the negroes set to work and four immense cables dangling from overhead were attached with hooks to the hubs of the great jewelled wheels. At a resounding "Hey-yah!" John felt the car being lifted slowly from the ground—up and up—clear of the tallest rocks on both sides—then higher, until he could see a wavy, moonlit valley stretched out before him in sharp contrast to the quagmire of rocks that they had just left. Only on one side was there still rock—and then suddenly there was no rock beside them or anywhere around.

It was apparent that they had surmounted some immense knife-blade of stone, projecting perpendicularly into the air. In a moment they were going down again, and finally with a soft bump they were landed upon the smooth earth.

"The worst is over," said Percy, squinting out of the window. "It's only five miles from here, and our own road—tapestry brick—all the way. This belongs to us. This is where the United States ends, father says."

"Are we in Canada?"

"We are not. We're in the middle of the Montana Rockies. But you are now on the only five square miles of land in the country that's never been surveyed."

"Why hasn't it? Did they forget it?"

"No," said Percy, grinning, "they tried to do it three times. The first time my grandfather corrupted a whole department of the State survey; the second time he had the official maps of the United States tinkered with—that held them for fifteen years. The last time was harder. My father fixed it so that their compasses were in the strongest magnetic field ever artificially set up. He had a whole set of surveying instruments made with a slight defection that would allow for this territory not to appear, and he substituted them for the ones that were to be used. Then he had a river deflected and he had what looked like a village built up on its banks—so that they'd see it, and think it was a town ten miles farther up the valley. There's only one thing my father's afraid of," he concluded, "only one thing in the world that could be used to find us out."

"What's that?"

Percy sank his voice to a whisper.

"Aeroplanes," he breathed. "We've got half a dozen anti-aircraft guns and we've arranged it so far—but there've been a few deaths and a great many prisoners. Not that we mind *that*, you know, father and I, but it upsets mother and the girls, and there's always the chance that sometime we won't be able to arrange it."

Shreds and tatters of chinchilla, courtesy clouds in the green moon's heaven, were passing the green moon like precious Eastern stuffs paraded for the inspection of some Tartar Khan. It seemed to John that it was day, and that he was looking at some lads sailing above him in the air, showering down tracts and patent medicine circulars, with their messages of hope for despairing, rock-bound hamlets. It seemed to him that he could see them look down out of the clouds and stare—and stare at whatever there was to stare at in this place whither he was bound—What then? Were they induced to land by some insidious device to be immured far from patent medicines and from tracts until the judgment day—or, should they fail to fall into the trap, did a quick puff of smoke and the sharp round of a splitting shell bring them drooping to earth—and "upset" Percy's mother and sisters. John shook his head and the wraith of a hollow laugh issued silently from his parted lips. What desperate transaction lay hidden here? What a moral expedient of a bizarre Croesus? What terrible and golden mystery?...

The chinchilla clouds had drifted past now and outside the Montana night was bright as day. The tapestry brick of the road was smooth to the tread of the great tires as they rounded a still, moonlit lake; they passed into darkness for a moment, a pine grove, pungent and cool, then they came out into a broad avenue of lawn, and John's exclamation of pleasure was simultaneous with Percy's taciturn "We're home."

Full in the light of the stars, an exquisite château rose from the borders of the lake, climbed in marble radiance half the height of an adjoining mountain, then melted in grace, in perfect symmetry, in translucent feminine languor, into the massed darkness of a forest of pine. The many towers, the slender tracery of the sloping parapets, the chiselled wonder of a thousand yellow windows with their oblongs and hectagons and triangles of golden light, the shattered softness of the intersecting planes of star-shine and blue shade, all trembled on John's spirit like a chord of music. On one of the towers, the tallest, the blackest at its base, an arrangement of exterior lights at the top made a sort of floating fairyland—and as John gazed up in warm enchantment the faint acciaccare sound of violins drifted down in a rococo harmony that was like nothing he had ever beard before. Then in a moment the car stopped before wide, high marble steps around which the night air was fragrant with a host of flowers. At the top of the steps two great doors swung silently open and amber light flooded out upon the darkness, silhouetting the figure of an exquisite lady with black, high-piled hair, who held out her arms toward them.

"Mother," Percy was saying, "this is my friend, John Unger, from Hades."

Afterward John remembered that first night as a daze of many colors, of quick sensory impressions, of music soft as a voice in love, and of the beauty of things, lights and shadows, and motions and faces. There was a white-haired man who stood drinking a many-hued cordial from a crystal thimble set on a golden stem. There was a girl with a flowery face, dressed like Titania with braided sapphires in her hair. There was a room where the solid, soft gold of the walls yielded to the pressure of his hand, and a room that was like a platonic conception of the ultimate prison—ceiling, floor, and all, it was lined with an unbroken mass of diamonds, diamonds of every size and shape, until, lit with tall violet lamps in the corners, it dazzled the eyes with a whiteness that could be compared only with itself, beyond human wish or dream.

Through a maze of these rooms the two boys wandered. Sometimes the floor under their feet would flame in brilliant patterns from lighting below, patterns of barbaric clashing colors, of pastel delicacy, of sheer whiteness, or of subtle and intricate mosaic, surely from some mosque on the Adriatic Sea. Sometimes beneath layers of thick crystal he would see blue or green water swirling, inhabited by vivid fish and growths of rainbow foliage. Then they would be treading on furs of every texture and color or along corridors of palest ivory, unbroken as though carved complete from the gigantic tusks of dinosaurs extinct before the age of man....

Then a hazily remembered transition, and they were at dinner—where each plate was of two almost imperceptible layers of solid diamond between which was curiously worked a filigree of emerald design, a shaving sliced from green air. Music, plangent and unobtrusive, drifted down through far corridors—his chair, feathered and curved insidiously to his back, seemed to engulf and overpower him as he drank his first glass of port. He tried drowsily to answer a question that had been asked him, but the honeyed luxury that clasped his body added to the illusion of sleep—jewels, fabrics, wines, and metals blurred before his eyes into a sweet mist....

"Yes," he replied with a polite effort, "it certainly is hot enough for me down there."

He managed to add a ghostly laugh; then, without movement, without resistance, he seemed to float off and away, leaving an iced dessert that was pink as a dream....He fell asleep.

When he awoke he knew that several hours had passed. He was in a great quiet room with ebony walls and a dull illumination that was too faint, too subtle, to be called a light. His young host was standing over him.

"You fell asleep at dinner," Percy was saying. "I nearly did, too—it was such a treat to be comfortable again after this year of school. Servants undressed and bathed you while you were sleeping."

"Is this a bed or a cloud?" sighed John. "Percy, Percy—before you go, I want to apologize."

"For what?"

"For doubting you when you said you had a diamond as big as the Ritz-Carlton Hotel."

Percy smiled.

"I thought you didn't believe me. It's that mountain, you know."

"What mountain?"

"The mountain the château rests on. It's not very big, for a mountain. But except about fifty feet of sod and gravel on top it's solid diamond. *One* diamond, one cubic mile without a flaw. Aren't you listening? Say——"

But John T. Unger had again fallen asleep.

3

Morning. As he awoke he perceived drowsily that the room had at the same moment become dense with sunlight. The ebony panels of one wall had slid aside on a sort of track, leaving his chamber half open to the day. A large negro in a white uniform stood beside his bed.

"Good-evening," muttered John, summoning his brains from the wild places.

"Good-morning, sir. Are you ready for your bath, sir? Oh, don't get up—I'll put you in, if you'll just unbutton your pajamas—there. Thank you, sir."

John lay quietly as his pajamas were removed—he was amused and delighted; he expected to be lifted like a child by this black Gargantua who was tending him, but nothing of the sort happened; instead he felt the bed tilt up slowly on its side—he began to roll, startled at first, in the direction of the wall, but when he reached the wall its drapery gave way, and sliding two yards farther down a fleecy incline he plumped gently into water the same temperature as his body.

He looked about him. The runway or rollway on which he had arrived had folded gently back into place. He had been projected into another chamber and was sitting in a sunken bath with his head just above the level of the floor. All about him, lining the walls of the room and the sides and bottom of the bath itself, was a blue aquarium, and gazing through the crystal surface on which he sat, he could see fish swimming among amber lights and even gliding without curiosity past his outstretched toes, which were separated from them only by the thickness of the crystal. From overhead, sunlight came down through sea-green glass.

"I suppose, sir, that you'd like hot rosewater and soapsuds this morning, sir—and perhaps cold saltwater to finish."

The negro was standing beside him.

"Yes," agreed John, smiling inanely, "as you please." Any idea of ordering this bath according to his own meagre standards of living would have been priggish and not a little wicked.

The negro pressed a button and a warm rain began to fall, apparently from overhead, but really, so John discovered after a moment, from a fountain arrangement nearby. The water turned to a pale rose color and jets of liquid soap spurted into it from four miniature walrus heads at the corners of the bath. In a moment a dozen little paddle-wheels, fixed to the sides, had churned the mixture into a radiant rainbow of pink foam which enveloped him softly with its delicious lightness, and burst in shining, rosy bubbles here and there about him.

"Shall I turn on the moving-picture machine, sir?" suggested the negro deferentially. "There's a good one-reel comedy in this machine today, or I can put in a serious piece in a moment, if you prefer it.

"No, thanks," answered John, politely but firmly. He was enjoying his bath too much to desire any distraction. But distraction came. In a moment he was listening intently to the sound of flutes from just outside, flutes dripping a melody that was like a waterfall, cool and green as the room itself, accompanying a frothy piccolo, in play more fragile than the lace of suds that covered and charmed him.

After a cold saltwater bracer and a cold fresh finish, he stepped out and into a fleecy robe, and upon a couch covered with the same material he was rubbed with oil, alcohol, and spice. Later he sat in a voluptuous chair while he was shaved and his hair was trimmed.

"Mr. Percy is waiting in your sitting-room," said the negro, when these operations were finished. "My name is Gygsum, Mr. Unger, sir.

I am to see to Mr. Unger every morning."

John walked out into the brisk sunshine of his living-room, where he found breakfast waiting for him and Percy, gorgeous in white kid knickerbockers, smoking in an easy chair.

4

This is a story of the Washington family as Percy sketched it for John during breakfast.

The father of the present Mr. Washington had been a Virginian, a direct descendant of George Washington, and Lord Baltimore. At the close of the Civil War he was a twenty-five-year-old Colonel with a played-out plantation and about a thousand dollars in gold.

Fitz-Norman Culpepper Washington, for that was the young Colonel's name, decided to present the Virginia estate to his younger brother and go West. He selected two dozen of the most faithful blacks, who, of course, worshipped him, and bought twenty-five tickets to the West, where he intended to take out land in their names and start a sheep and cattle ranch.

When he had been in Montana for less than a month and things were going very poorly indeed, he stumbled on his great discovery. He had lost his way when riding in the hills, and after a day without food he began to grow hungry. As he was without his rifle, he was forced to pursue a squirrel, and, in the course of the pursuit he noticed that it was carrying something shiny in its mouth. Just before it vanished into its hole—for Providence did not intend that this squirrel should alleviate his hunger—it dropped its burden. Sitting down to consider the situation Fitz-Norman's eye was caught by a gleam in the grass beside him. In ten seconds he had completely lost his appetite and gained one hundred thousand dollars. The squirrel, which had refused with annoying persistence to become food, had made him a present of a large and perfect diamond.

Late that night he found his way to camp and twelve hours later all the males among his darkies were back by the squirrel hole digging furiously at the side of the mountain. He told them he had discovered a rhinestone mine, and, as only one or two of them had ever seen even a small diamond before, they believed him, without question.

When the magnitude of his discovery became apparent to him, he found himself in a quandary. The mountain was *a* diamond—it was literally nothing else but solid diamond. He filled four saddle bags full of glittering samples and started on horseback for St. Paul. There he managed to dispose of half a dozen small stones—when he tried a larger one a storekeeper fainted and Fitz-Norman was arrested as a public disturber. He escaped from jail and caught the train for New York, where he sold a few medium-sized diamonds and received in exchange about two hundred thousand dollars in gold. But he did not dare to produce any exceptional gems—in fact, he left New York just in time. Tremendous excitement had been created in jewelry circles, not so much by the size of his diamonds as by their appearance in the city from mysterious sources. Wild rumors became current that a diamond mine had been discovered in the Catskills, on the Jersey coast, on Long Island, beneath Washington Square. Excursion trains, packed with men carrying picks and shovels, began to leave New York hourly, bound for various neighboring El Dorados. But by that time young Fitz-Norman was on his way back to Montana.

By the end of a fortnight he had estimated that the diamond in the mountain was approximately equal in quantity to all the rest of the diamonds known to exist in the world. There was no valuing it by any regular computation, however, for it was *one solid diamond*—and if it were offered for sale not only would the bottom fall out of the market, but also, if the value should vary with its size in the usual arithmetical progression, there would not be enough gold in the world to buy a tenth part of it. And what could anyone do with a diamond that size?

It was an amazing predicament. He was, in one sense, the richest man that ever lived—and yet was he worth anything at all? If his secret should transpire there was no telling to what measures the Government might resort in order to prevent a panic, in gold as well as in jewels. They might take over the claim immediately and institute a monopoly.

There was no alternative—he must market his mountain in secret. He sent South for his younger brother and put him in charge of his colored following, darkies who had never realized that slavery was abolished. To make sure of this, he read them a proclamation that he had composed, which announced that General Forrest had reorganized the shattered Southern armies and defeated the North in one pitched battle. The negroes believed him implicitly. They passed a vote declaring it a good thing and held revival services immediately.

Fitz-Norman himself set out for foreign parts with one hundred thousand dollars and two trunks filled with rough diamonds of all sizes. He sailed for Russia in a Chinese junk and six months after his departure from Montana he was in St. Petersburg. He took obscure lodgings and called immediately upon the court jeweller, announcing that he had a diamond for the Czar. He remained in St. Petersburg for two weeks, in constant danger of being murdered, living from lodging to lodging, and afraid to visit his trunks more than three or four times during the whole fortnight.

On his promise to return in a year with larger and finer stones, he was allowed to leave for India. Before he left, however, the Court Treasurers had deposited to his credit, in American banks, the sum of fifteen million dollars—under four different aliases.

He returned to America in 1868, having been gone a little over two years. He had visited the capitals of twenty-two countries and talked with five emperors, eleven kings, three princes, a shah, a khan, and a sultan. At that time Fitz-Norman estimated his own wealth at one billion dollars. One fact worked consistently against the disclosure of his secret. No one of his larger diamonds remained in the public eye for a week before being invested with a history of enough fatalities, amours, revolutions, and wars to have occupied it from the days of the first Babylonian Empire.

From 1870 until his death in 1900, the history of Fitz-Norman Washington was a long epic in gold. There were side issues, of course—he evaded the surveys, he married a Virginia lady, by whom he had a single son, and he was compelled, due to a series of unfortunate complications, to murder his brother, whose unfortunate habit of drinking himself into an indiscreet stupor had several times endangered their safety. But very few other murders stained these happy years of progress and expansion.

Just before he died he changed his policy, and with all but a few million dollars of his outside wealth bought up rare minerals in bulk, which he deposited in the safety vaults of banks all over the world, marked as bric-à-brac. His son, Braddock Tarleton Washington, followed this policy on an even more tensive scale. The minerals were converted into the rarest of all elements—radium—so that the equivalent of a billion dollars in gold could be placed in a receptacle no bigger than a cigar box.

When Fitz-Norman had been dead three years his son, Braddock, decided that the business had gone far enough. The amount of wealth that he and his father had taken out of the mountain was beyond all exact computation. He kept a notebook in cipher in which he set down the approximate quantity of radium in each of the thousand banks he patronized, and recorded the alias under which it was held. Then he did a very simple thing—he sealed up the mine.

He sealed up the mine. What had been taken out of it would support all the Washingtons yet to be born in unparalleled luxury for generations. His one care must be the protection of his secret, lest in the possible panic attendant on its discovery he should be reduced with all the property-holders in the world to utter poverty.

This was the family among whom John T. Unger was staying. This was the story he heard in his silver-walled living-room the morning after his arrival.

5

After breakfast, John found his way out the great marble entrance, and looked curiously at the scene before him. The whole valley, from the diamond mountain to the steep granite cliff five miles away, still gave off a breath of golden haze which hovered idly above the fine sweep of lawns and lakes and gardens. Here and there clusters of elms made delicate groves of shade, contrasting strangely with the tough masses of pine forest that held the hills in a grip of dark-blue green. Even as John looked he saw three fawns in single file patter out from one clump about a half-mile away and disappear with awkward gaiety into the black-ribbed half-light of another. John would not have been surprised to see a goat-foot piping his way among the trees or to catch a glimpse of pink nymph-skin and flying yellow hair between the greenest of the green leaves.

In some such cool hope he descended the marble steps, disturbing faintly the sleep of two silky Russian wolfhounds at the bottom, and set off along a walk of white and blue brick that seemed to lead in no particular direction.

He was enjoying himself as much as he was able. It is youth's felicity as well as its insufficiency that it can never live in the present, but must always be measuring up the day against its own radiantly imagined future—flowers and gold, girls and stars, they are only prefigurations and prophecies of that incomparable, unattainable young dream.

John rounded a soft corner where the massed rosebushes filled the air with heavy scent, and struck off across a park toward a patch of moss under some trees. He had never lain upon moss, and he wanted to see whether it was really soft enough to justify the use of its name as an adjective. Then he saw a girl coming toward him over the grass. She was the most beautiful person he had ever seen.

She was dressed in a white little gown that came just below her knees, and a wreath of mignonettes clasped with blue slices of sapphire bound up her hair. Her pink bare feet scattered the dew before them as she came. She was younger than John—not more than sixteen.

"Hallo," she cried softly, "I'm Kismine."

She was much more than that to John already. He advanced toward her, scarcely moving as he drew near lest he should tread on her bare toes.

"You haven't met me," said her soft voice. Her blue eyes added, "Oh, but you've missed a great deal!"... "You met my sister, Jasmine, last night. I was sick with lettuce poisoning," went on her soft voice, and her eyes continued, "and when I'm sick I'm sweet—and when I'm well."

"You have made an enormous impression on me," said John's eyes, "and I'm not so slow myself"—"How do you do?" said his voice. "I hope you're better this morning."—"You darling," added his eyes tremulously.

John observed that they had been walking along the path. On her suggestion they sat down together upon the moss, the softness of which he failed to determine.

He was critical about women. A single defect—a thick ankle, a hoarse voice, a glass eye—was enough to make him utterly indifferent. And here for the first time in his life he was beside a girl who seemed to him the incarnation of physical perfection.

"Are you from the East?" asked Kismine with charming

interest.

"No," answered John simply. "I'm from Hades."

Either she had never heard of Hades, or she could think of no pleasant comment to make upon it, for she did not discuss it further.

"I'm going East to school this fall," she said. "D'you think I'll like it? I'm going to New York to Miss Bulge's. It's very strict, but you see over the weekends I'm going to live at home with the family in our New York house, because father heard that the girls had to go walking two by two."

"Your father wants you to be proud," observed John.

"We are," she answered, her eyes shining with dignity. "None of us has ever been punished. Father said we never should be. Once when my sister Jasmine was a little girl she pushed him downstairs and he just got up and limped away.

"Mother was—well, a little startled," continued Kismine, "when she heard that you were from—from where you *are* from, you know. She said that when she was a young girl—but then, you see, she's a Spaniard and old-fashioned."

"Do you spend much time out here?" asked John, to conceal the fact that he was somewhat hurt by this remark. It seemed an unkind allusion to his provincialism.

"Percy and Jasmine and I are here every summer, but next summer Jasmine is going to Newport. She's coming out in London a year from this fall. She'll be presented at court."

"Do you know," began John hesitantly, "you're much more sophisticated than I thought you were when I first saw you?"

"Oh, no, I'm not," she exclaimed hurriedly. "Oh, I wouldn't think of being. I think that sophisticated young people are *terribly* common, don't you? I'm not at all, really. If you say I am, I'm going to cry."

She was so distressed that her lip was trembling. John was impelled to protest:

"I didn't mean that; I only said it to tease you."

"Because I wouldn't mind if I *were*," she persisted, "but I'm *not*. I'm very innocent and girlish. I never smoke, or drink, or read anything except poetry. I know scarcely any mathematics or chemistry. I dress *very* simply—in fact, I scarcely dress at all. I think sophisticated is the last thing you can say about me. I believe that girls ought to enjoy their youths in a wholesome way."

"I do, too," said John, heartily,

Kismine was cheerful again. She smiled at him, and a still-born tear dripped from the corner of one blue eye.

"I like you," she whispered, intimately. "Are you going to spend all your time with Percy while you're here, or will you be nice to me? Just think—I'm absolutely fresh ground. I've never had a boy in love with me in all my life. I've never been allowed even to *see* boys alone—except Percy. I came all the way out here into this grove hoping to run into you, where the family wouldn't be around."

Deeply flattered, John bowed from the hips as he had been taught at dancing school in Hades.

"We'd better go now," said Kismine sweetly. "I have to be with mother at eleven. You haven't asked me to kiss you once. I thought boys always did that nowadays"

John drew himself up proudly.

"Some of them do," he answered, "but not me. Girls don't do that sort of thing—in Hades."

Side by side they walked back toward the house.

6

John stood facing Mr. Braddock Washington in the full sunlight. The elder man was about forty with a proud, vacuous face, intelligent eyes, and a robust figure. In the mornings he smelt of horses—the best horses. He carried a plain walking-stick of gray birch with a single large opal for a grip. He and Percy were showing John around.

"The slaves' quarters are there." His walking-stick indicated a cloister of marble on their left that ran in graceful Gothic along the side of the mountain. "In my youth I was distracted for a while from the business of life by a period of absurd idealism. During that time they lived in luxury. For instance, I equipped every one of their rooms with a tile bath."

"I suppose," ventured John, with an ingratiating laugh, "that they used the bathtubs to keep coal in. Mr. Schnlitzer-Murphy told me that once he——"

"The opinions of Mr. Schnlitzer-Murphy are of little importance, I should imagine," interrupted Braddock Washington, coldly. "My slaves did not keep coal in their bathtubs. They had orders to bathe every day, and they did. If they hadn't I might have ordered a sulphuric acid shampoo. I discontinued the baths for quite another reason. Several of them caught cold and died. Water is not good for certain races—except as a beverage."

John laughed, and then decided to nod his head in sober agreement. Braddock Washington made him uncomfortable.

"All these negroes are descendants of the ones my father brought North with him. There are about two hundred and fifty now. You notice that they've lived so long apart from the world that their original dialect has become an almost indistinguishable patois. We bring a few of them up to speak English—my secretary and two or three of the house servants.

"This is the golf course," he continued, as they strolled along the velvet winter grass. "It's all a green, you see—no fairway, no rough, no hazards."

He smiled pleasantly at John.

"Many men in the cage, father?" asked Percy suddenly.

Braddock Washington stumbled, and let forth an involuntary curse.

"One less than there should be," he ejaculated darkly—and then added after a moment, "We've had difficulties."

"Mother was telling me," exclaimed Percy, "that Italian teacher——"

"A ghastly error," said Braddock Washington angrily. "But of course there's a good chance that we may have got him. Perhaps he fell somewhere in the woods or stumbled over a cliff. And then there's always the probability that if he did get away his story wouldn't be believed. Nevertheless, I've had two dozen men looking for him in different towns around here."

"And no luck?"

"Some. Fourteen of them reported to my agent they'd each killed a man answering to that description, but of course it was probably only the reward they were after——"

He broke off. They had come to a large cavity in the earth about the circumference of a merry-go-round and covered by a strong iron grating. Braddock Washington beckoned to John, and pointed his cane down through the grating. John stepped to the edge and gazed. Immediately his ears were assailed by a wild clamor from below.

"Come on down to Hell!"

"Hallo, kiddo, how's the air up there?"

"Hey! Throw us a rope!"

"Got an old doughnut, Buddy, or a couple of second-hand sandwiches?"

"Say, fella, if you'll push down that guy you're with, we'll show you a quick disappearance scene."

"Paste him one for me, will you?"

It was too dark to see clearly into the pit below, but John could tell from the coarse optimism and rugged vitality of the remarks and voices that they proceeded from middle-class Americans of the more spirited type. Then Mr. Washington put out his cane and touched a button in the grass, and the scene below sprang into light.

"These are some adventurous mariners who had the misfortune to discover El Dorado," he remarked.

Below them there had appeared a large hollow in the earth shaped like the interior of a bowl. The sides were steep and apparently of polished glass, and on its slightly concave surface stood about two dozen men clad in the half costume, half uniform, of aviators. Their upturned faces, lit with wrath, with malice, with despair, with cynical humor, were covered by long growths of beard, but with the exception of a few who had pined perceptibly away, they seemed to be a well-fed, healthy lot.

Braddock Washington drew a garden chair to the edge of the pit and sat down.

"Well, how are you, boys?" he inquired genially.

A chorus of execration, in which all joined except a few too dispirited to cry out, rose up into the sunny air, but Braddock Washington heard it with unruffled composure. When its last echo had died away he spoke again.

"Have you thought up a way out of your difficulty?"

From here and there among them a remark floated up.

"We decided to stay here for love!"

"Bring us up there and we'll find us a way!"

Braddock Washington waited until they were again quiet. Then he said:

"I've told you the situation. I don't want you here. I wish to heaven I'd never seen you. Your own curiosity got you here, and any time that you can think of a way out which protects me and my interests I'll be glad to consider it. But so long as you confine your efforts to digging tunnels—yes, I know about the new one you've started—you won't get very far. This isn't as hard on you as you make it out, with all your howling for the loved ones at home. If you were the type who worried much about the loved ones at home, you'd never have taken up aviation."

A tall man moved apart from the others, and held up his hand to call his captor's attention to what he was about to say.

"Let me ask you a few questions!" he cried. "You pretend to be a fair-minded man."

"How absurd. How could a man of *my* position be fair-minded toward *you*? You might as well speak of a Spaniard being fair-minded toward a piece of steak."

At this harsh observation the faces of the two dozen steaks fell, but the tall man continued:

"All right!" he cried. "We've argued this out before. You're not a humanitarian and you're not fair-minded, but you're human—at least you say you are—and you ought to be able to put yourself in our place for long enough to think how—how—how——"

"How what?" demanded Washington, coldly.

"—how unnecessary——"

"Not to me."

"Well,—how cruel——"

"We've covered that. Cruelty doesn't exist where self-preservation is involved. You've been soldiers; you know that. Try another."

"Well, then, how stupid."

"There," admitted Washington, "I grant you that. But try to think of an alternative. I've offered to have all or any of you painlessly executed if you wish. I've offered to have your wives, sweethearts, children, and mothers kidnapped and brought out here. I'll enlarge your place down there and feed and clothe you the rest of your lives. If there was some method of producing permanent amnesia I'd have all of you operated on and released immediately, somewhere outside of my preserves. But that's as far as my ideas go."

"How about trusting us not to peach on you?" cried someone.

"You don't proffer that suggestion seriously," said Washington, with an expression of scorn. "I did take out one man to teach my daughter Italian. Last week he got away."

A wild yell of jubilation went up suddenly from two dozen throats and a pandemonium of joy ensued. The prisoners clog-danced and cheered and yodled and wrestled with one another in a sudden uprush of animal spirits. They even ran up the glass sides of the bowl as far as they could, and slid back to the bottom upon the natural cushions of their bodies. The tall man started a song in which they all joined——

> *"Oh, we'll hang the kaiser*
> *On a sour apple-tree——"*

Braddock Washington sat in inscrutable silence until the song was over.

"You see," he remarked, when he could gain a modicum of attention. "I bear you no ill-will. I like to see you enjoying yourselves. That's why I didn't tell you the whole story at once. The man—what was his name? Critchtichiello?—was shot by some of my agents in fourteen different places."

Not guessing that the places referred to were cities, the tumult of rejoicing subsided immediately.

"Nevertheless," cried Washington with a touch of anger, "he tried to run away. Do you expect me to take chances with any of you after an experience like that?"

Again a series of ejaculations went up.

"Sure!"

"Would your daughter like to learn Chinese?"

"Hey, I can speak Italian! My mother was a wop."

"Maybe she'd like t'learna speak N'Yawk!"

"If she's the little one with the big blue eyes I can teach her a lot of things better than Italian."

"I know some Irish songs—and I could hammer brass once't."

Mr. Washington reached forward suddenly with his cane and pushed the button in the grass so that the picture below went out instantly, and there remained only that great dark mouth covered dismally with the black teeth of the grating.

"Hey!" called a single voice from below, "you ain't goin' away without givin' us your blessing?"

But Mr. Washington, followed by the two boys, was already strolling on toward the ninth hole of the golf course, as though the pit and its contents were no more than a hazard over which his facile iron had triumphed with ease.

7

July under the lee of the diamond mountain was a month of blanket nights and of warm, glowing days. John and Kismine were in love. He did not know that the little gold football (inscribed with the legend *Pro deo et patria et St. Mida*) which he had given her rested on a platinum chain next to her bosom. But it did. And she for her part was not aware that a large sapphire which had dropped one day from her simple coiffure was stowed away tenderly in John's jewel box.

Late one afternoon when the ruby and ermine music room was quiet, they spent an hour there together. He held her hand and she gave him such a look that he whispered her name aloud. She bent toward him—then hesitated.

"Did you say 'Kismine'?" she asked softly, "or——"

She had wanted to be sure. She thought she might have misunderstood.

Neither of them had ever kissed before, but in the course of an hour it seemed to make little difference.

The afternoon drifted away. That night when a last breath of music drifted down from the highest tower, they each lay awake, happily dreaming over the separate minutes of the day. They had decided to be married as soon as possible.

8

Every day Mr. Washington and the two young men went hunting or fishing in the deep forests or played golf around the somnolent course—games which John diplomatically allowed his host to win—or swam in the mountain coolness of the lake. John found Mr.

Washington a somewhat exacting personality—utterly uninterested in any ideas or opinions except his own. Mrs. Washington was aloof and reserved at all times. She was apparently indifferent to her two daughters, and entirely absorbed in her son Percy, with whom she held interminable conversations in rapid Spanish at dinner.

Jasmine, the elder daughter, resembled Kismine in appearance—except that she was somewhat bow-legged, and terminated in large hands and feet—but was utterly unlike her in temperament. Her favorite books had to do with poor girls who kept house for widowed fathers. John learned from Kismine that Jasmine had never recovered from the shock and disappointment caused her by the termination of the World War, just as she was about to start for Europe as a canteen expert. She had even pined away for a time, and Braddock Washington had taken steps to promote a new war in the Balkans—but she had seen a photograph of some wounded Serbian soldiers and lost interest in the whole proceedings. But Percy and Kismine seemed to have inherited the arrogant attitude in all its harsh magnificence from their father. A chaste and consistent selfishness ran like a pattern through their every idea.

John was enchanted by the wonders of the château and the valley. Braddock Washington, so Percy told him, had caused to be kidnapped a landscape gardener, an architect, a designer of stage settings, and a French decadent poet left over from the last century. He had put his entire force of negroes at their disposal, guaranteed to supply them with any materials that the world could offer, and left them to work out some ideas of their own. But one by one they had shown their uselessness. The decadent poet had at once begun bewailing his separation from the boulevards in spring—he made some vague remarks about spices, apes, and ivories, but said nothing that was of any practical value. The stage designer on his part wanted to make the whole valley a series of tricks and sensational effects—a state of things that the Washingtons would soon have grown tired of. And as for the architect and the landscape gardener, they thought only in terms of convention. They must make this like this and that like that.

But they had, at least, solved the problem of what was to be done with them—they all went mad early one morning after spending the night in a single room trying to agree upon the location of a fountain, and were now confined comfortably in an insane asylum at Westport, Connecticut.

"But," inquired John curiously, "who did plan all your wonderful reception rooms and halls, and approaches and bathrooms——?"

"Well," answered Percy, "I blush to tell you, but it was a moving-picture fella. He was the only man we found who was used to playing with an unlimited amount of money, though he did tuck his napkin in his collar and couldn't read or write."

As August drew to a close John began to regret that he must soon go back to school. He and Kismine had decided to elope the following June.

"It would be nicer to be married here," Kismine confessed, "but of course I could never get father's permission to marry you at all. Next to that I'd rather elope. It's terrible for wealthy people to be married in America at present—they always have to send out bulletins to the press saying that they're going to be married in remnants, when what they mean is just a peck of old secondhand pearls and some used lace worn once by the Empress Eugénie."

"I know," agreed John fervently. "When I was visiting the Schnlitzer-Murphys, the eldest daughter, Gwendolyn, married a man whose father owns half of West Virginia. She wrote home saying what a tough struggle she was carrying on on his salary as a bank clerk—and then she ended up by saying that 'Thank God, I have four good maids anyhow, and that helps a little.'"

"It's absurd," commented Kismine—"Think of the millions and millions of people in the world, laborers and all, who get along with only two maids."

One afternoon late in August a chance remark of Kismine's changed the face of the entire situation, and threw John into a state of terror.

They were in their favorite grove, and between kisses John was indulging in some romantic forebodings which he fancied added poignancy to their relations.

"Sometimes I think we'll never marry," he said sadly. "You're too wealthy, too magnificent. No one as rich as you are can be like other girls. I should marry the daughter of some well-to-do wholesale hardware man from Omaha or Sioux City, and be content with her half-million."

"I knew the daughter of a wholesale hardware man once," remarked Kismine. "I don't think you'd have been contented with her. She was a friend of my sister's. She visited here."

"Oh, then you've had other guests?" exclaimed John in surprise.

Kismine seemed to regret her words.

"Oh, yes," she said hurriedly, "we've had a few."

"But aren't you—wasn't your father afraid they'd talk outside?"

"Oh, to some extent, to some extent," she answered, "Let's talk about something pleasanter."

But John's curiosity was aroused.

"Something pleasanter!" he demanded. "What's unpleasant about that? Weren't they nice girls?"

To his great surprise Kismine began to weep.

"Yes—th—that's the—the whole t-trouble. I grew qu-quite attached to some of them. So did Jasmine, but she kept inv-viting them anyway. I couldn't under*stand* it."

A dark suspicion was born in John's heart.

"Do you mean that they *told*, and your father had them—removed?"

"Worse than that," she muttered brokenly. "Father took no chances—and Jasmine kept writing them to come, and they had *such* a good time!"

She was overcome by a paroxysm of grief.

Stunned with the horror of this revelation, John sat there open-mouthed, feeling the nerves of his body twitter like so many sparrows perched upon his spinal column.

"Now, I've told you, and I shouldn't have," she said, calming suddenly and drying her dark blue eyes.

"Do you mean to say that your father had them *murdered* before they left?"

She nodded.

"In August usually—or early in September. It's only natural for us to get all the pleasure out of them that we can first."

"How abominable! How—why, I must be going crazy! Did you really admit that——"

"I did," interrupted Kismine, shrugging her shoulders. "We can't very well imprison them like those aviators, where they'd be a continual reproach to us every day. And it's always been made easier for Jasmine and me, because father had it done sooner than we expected. In that way we avoided any farewell scene——"

"So you murdered them! Uh!" cried John.

"It was done very nicely. They were drugged while they were asleep—and their families were always told that they died of scarlet fever in Butte."

"But—I fail to understand why you kept on inviting them!"

"I didn't," burst out Kismine. "I never invited one. Jasmine did. And they always had a very good time. She'd give them the nicest presents toward the last. I shall probably have visitors too—I'll harden up to it. We can't let such an inevitable thing as death stand in the way of enjoying life while we have it. Think how lonesome it'd be out here if we never had *any*one. Why, father and mother have sacrificed some of their best friends just as we have."

"And so," cried John accusingly, "and so you were letting me make love to you and pretending to return it, and talking about marriage, all the time knowing perfectly well that I'd never get out of here alive——"

"No," she protested passionately. "Not anymore. I did at first. You were here. I couldn't help that, and I thought your last days might as well be pleasant for both of us. But then I fell in love with you, and—and I'm honestly sorry you're going to—going to be put away—though I'd rather you'd be put away than ever kiss another girl."

"Oh, you would, would you?" cried John ferociously.

"Much rather. Besides, I've always heard that a girl can have more fun with a man whom she knows she can never marry. Oh, why did I tell you? I've probably spoiled your whole good time now, and we were really enjoying things when you didn't know it. I knew it would make things sort of depressing for you."

"Oh, you did, did you?" John's voice trembled with anger. "I've heard about enough of this. If you haven't any more pride and decency than to have an affair with a fellow that you know isn't much better than a corpse, I don't want to have any more to do with you!"

"You're not a corpse!" she protested in horror. "You're not a corpse! I won't have you saying that I kissed a corpse!"

"I said nothing of the sort!"

"You did! You said I kissed a corpse!"

"I didn't!"

Their voices had risen, but upon a sudden interruption they both subsided into immediate silence. Footsteps were coming along the path in their direction, and a moment later the rose bushes were parted displaying Braddock Washington, whose intelligent eyes set in his good-looking vacuous face were peering in at them.

"Who kissed a corpse?" he demanded in obvious disapproval.

"Nobody," answered Kismine quickly. "We were just joking."

"What are you two doing here, anyhow?" he demanded gruffly. "Kismine, you ought to be—to be reading or playing golf with your sister. Go read! Go play golf! Don't let me find you here when I come back!"

Then he bowed at John and went up the path.

"See?" said Kismine crossly, when he was out of hearing. "You've spoiled it all. We can never meet anymore. He won't let me meet you. He'd have you poisoned if he thought we were in love."

"We're not, anymore!" cried John fiercely, "so he can set his mind at rest upon that. Moreover, don't fool yourself that I'm going to stay around here. Inside of six hours I'll be over those mountains, if I have to gnaw a passage through them, and on my way East."

They had both got to their feet, and at this remark Kismine came close and put her arm through his.

"I'm going, too."

"You must be crazy——"

"Of course I'm going," she interrupted impatiently.

"You most certainly are not. You——"

"Very well," she said quietly, "we'll catch up with father now and talk it over with him."

Defeated, John mustered a sickly smile.

"Very well, dearest," he agreed, with pale and unconvincing affection, "we'll go together."

His love for her returned and settled placidly on his heart. She was his—she would go with him to share his dangers. He put his arms about her and kissed her fervently. After all she loved him; she had saved him, in fact.

Discussing the matter, they walked slowly back toward the château. They decided that since Braddock Washington had seen them together they had best depart the next night. Nevertheless, John's lips were unusually dry at dinner, and he nervously emptied a great spoonful of peacock soup into his left lung. He had to be carried into the turquoise and sable card-room and pounded on the back by one of the under-butlers, which Percy considered a great joke.

9

Long after midnight John's body gave a nervous jerk, he sat suddenly upright, staring into the veils of somnolence that draped the room. Through the squares of blue darkness that were his open windows, he had heard a faint far-away sound that died upon a bed of wind before identifying itself on his memory, clouded with uneasy dreams. But the sharp noise that had succeeded it was nearer, was just outside the room—the click of a turned knob, a footstep, a whisper, he could not tell; a hard lump gathered in the pit of his stomach, and his whole body ached in the moment that he strained agonizingly to hear. Then one of the veils seemed to dissolve, and he saw a vague figure standing by the door, a figure only faintly limned and blocked in upon the darkness, mingled so with the folds of the drapery as to seem distorted, like a reflection seen in a dirty pane of glass.

With a sudden movement of fright or resolution John pressed the button by his bedside, and the next moment he was sitting in the green sunken bath of the adjoining room, waked into alertness by the shock of the cold water which half filled it.

He sprang out, and, his wet pajamas scattering a heavy trickle of water behind him, ran for the aquamarine door which he knew led out onto the ivory landing of the second floor. The door opened noiselessly. A single crimson lamp burning in a great dome above lit the magnificent sweep of the carved stairways with a poignant beauty. For a moment John hesitated, appalled by the silent splendor massed about him, seeming to envelop in its gigantic folds and contours the solitary drenched little figure shivering upon the ivory landing. Then simultaneously two things happened. The door of his own sitting-room swung open, precipitating three naked negroes into the hall—and, as John swayed in wild terror toward the stairway, another door slid back in the wall on the other side of the corridor, and John saw

Braddock Washington standing in the lighted lift, wearing a fur coat and a pair of riding boots which reached to his knees and displayed, above, the glow of his rose-colored pajamas.

On the instant the three negroes—John had never seen any of them before, and it flashed through his mind that they must be the professional executioners—paused in their movement toward John, and turned expectantly to the man in the lift, who burst out with an imperious command:

"Get in here! All three of you! Quick as hell!"

Then, within the instant, the three negroes darted into the cage, the oblong of light was blotted out as the lift door slid shut, and John was again alone in the hall. He slumped weakly down against an ivory stair.

It was apparent that something portentous had occurred, something which, for the moment at least, had postponed his own petty disaster. What was it? Had the negroes risen in revolt? Had the aviators forced aside the iron bars of the grating? Or had the men of Fish stumbled blindly through the hills and gazed with bleak, joyless eyes upon the gaudy valley? John did not know. He heard a faint whir of air as the lift whizzed up again, and then, a moment later, as it descended. It was probable that Percy was hurrying to his father's assistance, and it occurred to John that this was his opportunity to join Kismine and plan an immediate escape. He waited until the lift had been silent for several minutes; shivering a little with the night cool that whipped in through his wet pajamas, he returned to his room and dressed himself quickly. Then he mounted a long flight of stairs and turned down the corridor carpeted with Russian sable which led to Kismine's suite.

The door of her sitting-room was open and the lamps were lighted. Kismine, in an angora kimono, stood near the window of the room in a listening attitude, and as John entered noiselessly she turned toward him.

"Oh, it's you!" she whispered, crossing the room to him. "Did you hear them?"

I heard your father's slaves in my——"

"No," she interrupted excitedly. "Aeroplanes!"

"Aeroplanes? Perhaps that was the sound that woke me."

"There're at least a dozen. I saw one a few moments ago dead against the moon. The guard back by the cliff fired his rifle and that's what roused father. We're going to open on them right away."

"Are they here on purpose?"

"Yes—it's that Italian who got away——"

Simultaneously with her last word, a succession of sharp cracks tumbled in through the open window. Kismine uttered a little cry, took a penny with fumbling fingers from a box on her dresser, and ran to one of the electric lights. In an instant the entire château was in darkness—she had blown out the fuse.

"Come on!" she cried to him. "We'll go up to the roof garden, and watch it from there!"

Drawing a cape about her, she took his hand, and they found their way out the door. It was only a step to the tower lift, and as she pressed the button that shot them upward he put his arms around her in the darkness and kissed her mouth. Romance had come to John Unger at last. A minute later they had stepped out upon the star-white platform. Above, under the misty moon, sliding in and out of the patches of cloud that eddied below it, floated a dozen dark-winged bodies in a constant circling course. From here and there in the valley flashes of fire leaped toward them, followed by sharp detonations. Kismine clapped her hands with pleasure, which, a moment later, turned to dismay as the aeroplanes, at some prearranged signal, began to release their bombs and the whole of the valley became a panorama of deep reverberate sound and lurid light.

Before long the aim of the attackers became concentrated upon the points where the anti-aircraft guns were situated, and one of them was almost immediately reduced to a giant cinder to lie smouldering in a park of rose bushes.

"Kismine," begged John, "you'll be glad when I tell you that this attack came on the eve of my murder. If I hadn't heard that guard shoot off his gun back by the pass I should now be stone dead——"

"I can't hear you!" cried Kismine, intent on the scene before her. "You'll have to talk louder!"

"I simply said," shouted John, "that we'd better get out before they begin to shell the château!"

Suddenly the whole portico of the negro quarters cracked asunder, a geyser of flame shot up from under the colonnades, and great fragments of jagged marble were hurled as far as the borders of the lake.

"There go fifty thousand dollars' worth of slaves," cried Kismine, "at pre-war prices. So few Americans have any respect for property."

John renewed his efforts to compel her to leave. The aim of the aeroplanes was becoming more precise minute by minute, and only two of the anti-aircraft guns were still retaliating. It was obvious that the garrison, encircled with fire, could not hold out much longer.

"Come on!" cried John, pulling Kismine's arm, "we've got to go. Do you realize that those aviators will kill you without question if they find you?"

She consented reluctantly.

"We'll have to wake Jasmine!" she said, as they hurried toward the lift. Then she added in a sort of childish delight: "We'll be poor, won't we? Like people in books. And I'll be an orphan and utterly free. Free and poor! What fun!" She stopped and raised her lips to him in a delighted kiss.

"It's impossible to be both together," said John grimly. "People have found that out. And I should choose to be free as preferable of the two. As an extra caution you'd better dump the contents of your jewel box into your pockets."

Ten minutes later the two girls met John in the dark corridor and they descended to the main floor of the château. Passing for the last time through the magnificence of the splendid halls, they stood for a moment out on the terrace, watching the burning negro quarters and the flaming embers of two planes which had fallen on the other side of the lake. A solitary gun was still keeping up a sturdy popping, and the attackers seemed timorous about descending lower, but sent their thunderous fireworks in a circle around it, until any chance shot might annihilate its Ethiopian crew.

John and the two sisters passed down the marble steps, turned sharply to the left, and began to ascend a narrow path that wound like a garter about the diamond mountain. Kismine knew a heavily wooded spot halfway up where they could lie concealed and yet be able to observe the wild night in the valley—finally to make an escape, when it should be necessary, along a secret path laid in a rocky gully.

10

It was three o'clock when they attained their destination. The obliging and phlegmatic Jasmine fell off to sleep immediately, leaning against the trunk of a large tree, while John and Kismine sat, his arm around her, and watched the desperate ebb and flow of the dying battle among the ruins of a vista that had been a garden spot that morning. Shortly after four o'clock the last remaining gun gave out a clanging sound and went out of action in a swift tongue of red smoke. Though the moon was down, they saw that the flying bodies were circling closer to the earth. When the planes had made certain that the beleaguered possessed no further resources, they would land and the dark and glittering reign of the Washingtons would be over.

With the cessation of the firing the valley grew quiet. The embers of the two aeroplanes glowed like the eyes of some monster crouching in the grass. The château stood dark and silent, beautiful without light as it had been beautiful in the sun, while the woody rattles of Nemesis filled the air above with a growing and receding complaint. Then John perceived that Kismine, like her sister, had fallen sound asleep.

It was long after four when he became aware of footsteps along the path they had lately followed, and he waited in breathless silence until the persons to whom they belonged had passed the vantage-point he occupied. There was a faint stir in the air now that was not of human origin, and the dew was cold; he knew that the dawn would break soon. John waited until the steps had gone a safe distance up the mountain and were inaudible. Then he followed. About halfway to the steep summit the trees fell away and a hard saddle of rock spread itself over the diamond beneath. Just before he reached this point he slowed down his pace, warned by an animal sense that there was life just ahead of him. Coming to a high boulder, he lifted his head gradually above its edge. His curiosity was rewarded; this is what he saw:

Braddock Washington was standing there motionless, silhouetted against the gray sky without sound or sign of life. As the dawn came up out of the east, lending a cold green color to the earth, it brought the solitary figure into insignificant contrast with the new day.

While John watched, his host remained for a few moments absorbed in some inscrutable contemplation; then he signalled to the two negroes who crouched at his feet to lift the burden which lay between them. As they struggled upright, the first yellow beam of the sun struck through the innumerable prisms of an immense and exquisitely chiselled diamond—and a white radiance was kindled that glowed upon the air like a fragment of the morning star. The bearers staggered beneath its weight for a moment—then their rippling muscles caught and hardened under the wet shine of the skins and the three figures were again motionless in their defiant impotency before the heavens.

After a while the white man lifted his head and slowly raised his arms in a gesture of attention, as one who would call a great crowd to hear—but there was no crowd, only the vast silence of the mountain and the sky, broken by faint bird voices down among the trees. The figure on the saddle of rock began to speak ponderously and with an inextinguishable pride.

"You—out there—!" he cried in a trembling voice.

"You—there—!" He paused, his arms still uplifted, his head held attentively as though he were expecting an answer. John strained his eyes to see whether there might be men coming down the mountain, but the mountain was bare of human life. There was only sky and a mocking flute of wind along the treetops. Could Washington be praying? For a moment John wondered. Then the illusion passed—there was something in the man's whole attitude antithetical to prayer.

"Oh, you above there!"

The voice was become strong and confident. This was no forlorn supplication. If anything, there was in it a quality of monstrous condescension.

"You there——" Words, too quickly uttered to be understood, flowing one into the other.... John listened breathlessly, catching a phrase here and there, while the voice broke off, resumed, broke off again—now strong and argumentative, now colored with a slow, puzzled impatience. Then a conviction commenced to dawn on the single listener, and as realization crept over him a spray of quick blood rushed through his arteries. Braddock Washington was offering a bribe to God!

That was it—there was no doubt. The diamond in the arms of his slaves was some advance sample, a promise of more to follow.

That, John perceived after a time, was the thread running through his sentences. Prometheus Enriched was calling to witness forgotten sacrifices, forgotten rituals, prayers obsolete before the birth of Christ. For a while his discourse took the form of reminding God of this gift or that which Divinity had deigned to accept from men—great churches if he would rescue cities from the plague, gifts of myrrh and gold, of human lives and beautiful women and captive armies, of children and queens, of beasts of the forest and field, sheep and goats, harvests and cities, whole conquered lands that had been offered up in lust or blood for His appeasal, buying a meed's worth of alleviation from the Divine wrath—and now he, Braddock Washington, Emperor of Diamonds, king and priest of the age of gold, arbiter of splendor and luxury, would offer up a treasure such as princes before him had never dreamed of, offer it up not in suppliance, but in pride.

He would give to God, he continued, getting down to specifications, the greatest diamond in the world. This diamond would be cut with many more thousand facets than there were leaves on a tree, and yet the whole diamond would be shaped with the perfection of a stone no bigger than a fly. Many men would work upon it for many years. It would be set in a great dome of beaten gold, wonderfully carved and equipped with gates of opal and crusted sapphire. In the middle would be hollowed out a chapel presided over by an altar of iridescent, decomposing, ever-changing radium which would burn out the eyes of any worshipper who lifted up his head from prayer—and on this altar there would be slain for the amusement of the Divine Benefactor any victim He should choose, even though it should be the greatest and most powerful man alive.

In return he asked only a simple thing, a thing that for God would be absurdly easy—only that matters should be as they were yesterday at this hour and that they should so remain. So very simple! Let but the heavens open, swallowing these men and their aeroplanes—and then close again. Let him have his slaves once more, restored to life and well.

There was no one else with whom he had ever needed to treat or bargain.

He doubted only whether he had made his bribe big enough. God had His price, of course. God was made in man's image, so it had been said: He must have His price. And the price would be rare—no cathedral whose building consumed many years, no pyramid constructed by ten thousand workmen, would be like this cathedral, this pyramid.

He paused here. That was his proposition. Everything would be up to specifications, and there was nothing vulgar in his assertion that it would be cheap at the price. He implied that Providence could take it or leave it.

As he approached the end his sentences became broken, became short and uncertain, and his body seemed tense, seemed strained to catch the slightest pressure or whisper of life in the spaces around him. His hair had turned gradually white as he talked, and now he lifted his head high to the heavens like a prophet of old—magnificently mad.

Then, as John stared in giddy fascination, it seemed to him that a curious phenomenon took place somewhere around him. It was as though the sky had darkened for an instant, as though there had been a sudden murmur in a gust of wind, a sound of far-away trumpets, a sighing like the rustle of a great silken robe—for a time the whole of nature round about partook of this darkness; the birds' song ceased; the trees were still, and far over the mountain there was a mutter of dull, menacing thunder.

That was all. The wind died along the tall grasses of the valley. The dawn and the day resumed their place in a time, and the risen sun sent hot waves of yellow mist that made its path bright before it. The leaves laughed in the sun, and their laughter shook the trees until each bough was like a girl's school in fairyland. God had refused to accept the bribe.

For another moment John watched the triumph of the day. Then, turning, he saw a flutter of brown down by the lake, then another flutter, then another, like the dance of golden angels alighting from the clouds. The aeroplanes had come to earth.

John slid off the boulder and ran down the side of the mountain to the clump of trees, where the two girls were awake and waiting for him. Kismine sprang to her feet, the jewels in her pockets jingling, a question on her parted lips, but instinct told John that there was no time for words. They must get off the mountain without losing a moment. He seized a hand of each, and in silence they threaded the tree-trunks, washed with light now and with the rising mist. Behind them from the valley came no sound at all, except the complaint of the peacocks far away and the pleasant undertone of morning.

When they had gone about half a mile, they avoided the park land and entered a narrow path that led over the next rise of ground. At the highest point of this they paused and turned around. Their eyes rested upon the mountainside they had just left—oppressed by some dark sense of tragic impendency.

Clear against the sky a broken, white-haired man was slowly descending the steep slope, followed by two gigantic and emotionless negroes, who carried a burden between them which still flashed and glittered in the sun. Halfway down two other figures joined them—John could see that they were Mrs. Washington and her son, upon whose arm she leaned. The aviators had clambered from their machines to the sweeping lawn in front of the château, and with rifles in hand were starting up the diamond mountain in skirmishing formation.

But the little group of five which had formed farther up and was engrossing all the watchers' attention had stopped upon a ledge of rock. The negroes stooped and pulled up what appeared to be a trapdoor in the side of the mountain. Into this they all disappeared, the white-haired man first, then his wife and son, finally the two negroes, the glittering tips of whose jewelled headdresses caught the sun for a moment before the trapdoor descended and engulfed them all.

Kismine clutched John's arm.

"Oh," she cried wildly, "where are they going? What are they going to do?"

"It must be some underground way of escape——"

A little scream from the two girls interrupted his sentence.

"Don't you see?" sobbed Kismine hysterically. "The mountain is wired!"

Even as she spoke John put up his hands to shield his sight. Before their eyes the whole surface of the mountain had changed suddenly to a dazzling burning yellow, which showed up through the jacket of turf as light shows through a human hand. For a moment the intolerable glow continued, and then like an extinguished filament it disappeared, revealing a black waste from which blue smoke arose slowly, carrying off with it what remained of vegetation and of human flesh. Of the aviators there was left neither blood nor bone—they were consumed as completely as the five souls who had gone inside.

Simultaneously, and with an immense concussion, the château literally threw itself into the air, bursting into flaming fragments as it rose, and then tumbling back upon itself in a smoking pile that lay projecting half into the water of the lake. There was no fire—what smoke there was drifted off mingling with the sunshine, and for a few minutes longer a powdery dust of marble drifted from the great featureless pile that had once been the house of jewels. There was no more sound and the three people were alone in the valley.

11

At sunset John and his two companions reached the huge cliff which had marked the boundaries of the Washington's dominion, and looking back found the valley tranquil and lovely in the dusk. They sat down to finish the food which Jasmine had brought with her in a basket.

"There!" she said, as she spread the tablecloth and put the sandwiches in a neat pile upon it. "Don't they look tempting? I always think that food tastes better outdoors."

"With that remark," remarked Kismine, "Jasmine enters the middle class."

"Now," said John eagerly, "turn out your pocket and let's see what jewels you brought along. If you made a good selection we three ought to live comfortably all the rest of our lives."

Obediently Kismine put her hand in her pocket and tossed two handfuls of glittering stones before him. "Not so bad," cried John enthusiastically. "They aren't very big, but-Hello!" His expression changed as he held one of them up to the declining sun. "Why, these aren't diamonds! There's something the matter!"

"By golly!" exclaimed Kismine, with a startled look. "What an idiot I am!"

"Why, these are rhinestones!" cried John.

"I know." She broke into a laugh. "I opened the wrong drawer. They belonged on the dress of a girl who visited Jasmine. I got her to give them to me in exchange for diamonds. I'd never seen anything but precious stones before."

"And this is what you brought?"

"I'm afraid so." She fingered the brilliants wistfully. "I think I like these better. I'm a little tired of diamonds."

"Very well," said John gloomily. "We'll have to live in Hades. And you will grow old telling incredulous women that you got the wrong drawer. Unfortunately your father's bank-books were consumed with him."

"Well, what's the matter with Hades?"

"If I come home with a wife at my age my father is just as liable as not to cut me off with a hot coal, as they say down there."

Jasmine spoke up.

"I love washing," she said quietly. "I have always washed my own handkerchiefs. I'll take in laundry and support you both."

"Do they have washwomen in Hades?" asked Kismine innocently.

"Of course," answered John. "It's just like anywhere else."

"I thought—perhaps it was too hot to wear any clothes."

John laughed.

"Just try it!" he suggested. "They'll run you out before you're half started."

"Will father be there?" she asked.

John turned to her in astonishment.

"Your father is dead," he replied somberly. "Why should he go to Hades? You have it confused with another place that was abolished long ago."

After supper they folded up the tablecloth and spread their blankets for the night.

"What a dream it was," Kismine sighed, gazing up at the stars. "How strange it seems to be here with one dress and a penniless fiancé!

"Under the stars," she repeated. "I never noticed the stars before. I always thought of them as great big diamonds that belonged to someone. Now they frighten me. They make me feel that it was all a dream, all my youth."

"It *was* a dream," said John quietly. "Everybody's youth is a dream, a form of chemical madness."

"How pleasant then to be insane!"

"So I'm told," said John gloomily. "I don't know any longer. At any rate, let us love for a while, for a year or so, you and me. That's a form of divine drunkenness that we can all try. There are only diamonds in the whole world, diamonds and perhaps the shabby gift of disillusion. Well, I have that last and I will make the usual nothing of it." He shivered. "Turn up your coat collar, little girl, the night's full of chill and you'll get pneumonia. His was a great sin who first invented consciousness. Let us lose it for a few hours."

So wrapping himself in his blanket he fell off to sleep.

Made in the USA
Middletown, DE
28 January 2021